Monster in the Mirror

Written by Jean Ure

Illustrated by Sholto Walker

Chapter 1

This is the story of Woffles and Stretch. Woffles was a dog, very big and woolly. Stretch was a cat, very smooth and slinky.

Stretch was called Stretch because he liked to

stre-e-e-e-e-e-tch.

Upwards, downwards, even backwards in a circle. He was a very stretchy sort of cat.

Woffles was called Woffles because he liked to woffle.
He woffled around the garden. He woffled around
the park. He was a real woffle hound.

Woffles and Stretch lived in a house with their People.
Woffles and Stretch loved their People and their People
loved them.

Woffles and Stretch were very happy until one day, the People came home carrying Something in a Box.

"See what we've got!" they cried.

Stretch opened an eye and yawned. But Woffles went running to look. What had the People brought? Was it food?

No! Woffles screeched to a halt. It was a creature.

It was *a cat!*

She was small and black.

"Isn't she cute?" cooed the People. "Come and say hello!"

Stretch slid off the washing machine. He picked his way s-l-o-w-l-y across the kitchen floor.

Woffles crept after him.

"Tsssss!" went the new cat, showing her claws.

"Woof!" Woffles sprang backwards in alarm. All his fur stood on end.

Stretch stayed where he was. He arched his back.

"Watch it!" he hissed. No strange cat came into *his* house and spat at him.

"Now, Stretch," said the People, "can't you see she's frightened?"

The new cat didn't look frightened!

Woffles was frightened! He stood in the corner, shaking.

"What a big baby," laughed the People.
"You're twice the size of this poor little mite!"

The poor little mite held up a paw.
All its nails were stuck out like pins
on a pincushion.

"I wish it hadn't come," thought Woffles.

Stretch just glinted out of his green eyes.
That cat had better behave, or there'd be TROUBLE.

Chapter 2

The new cat was called Muffy. Her manners were quite dreadful.

She spat and she hissed. She hissed and she spat. She made poor Woffles' life a misery.

She didn't hiss or spit at the People. Oh, no! She was too clever for that. She sat on the People's laps and purred. The People thought she was a real sweetie!

Muffy didn't hiss at Stretch, either. She tried it just once, but Stretch spat back and bopped her with his paw. "Watch it!" he hissed.

Muffy didn't like it when Stretch bopped her. So she left him alone and went to spit at Woffles, instead.

Woffles was such a big softie. Muffy bullied him all day long.

She lay in wait for him, in dark corners. She snatched at his tail. She clawed at his ears. Woffles couldn't eat his dinner in peace.

He couldn't lie on the sofa and snooze.

He couldn't even woffle about the garden, smelling interesting smells.

Poor Woffles! He didn't do any of the doggy things that he'd done before. He just hid beneath the kitchen table, or sat trembling in the garden, too scared to come in.

The People told him he was a big daft mutt, as they carried him in from the garden. "Fancy being scared of a little thing like that!"

Muffy became quite puffed up. She paraded about the house with her tail in the air and a wicked grin on her face.
All the time she was planning new ways to torment poor Woffles ...

As for Stretch, he just slept and ate, and groomed and stretched, and didn't lift a paw. Why should he? Nobody was bullying him.

Chapter 3

One Sunday, the People went to visit friends. "Be good," they told the animals, "we'll be back at dinner time."

The People jumped in their car and drove off.

Woffles watched through the window. He didn't feel safe with Muffy now that the People had gone out.

Stretch didn't mind. He was happy snoozing on top of the television.

Woffles jumped down from the window seat. He looked around nervously for Muffy. Where was she?

She was nowhere to be seen.

Woffles clambered on to the sofa. He gave a deep sigh and settled down to sleep. He was in the middle of a beautiful dream when ...

Something dropped on him. Something round. And black. And prickly. Something like a big furry pincushion ...

Woffles gave a yelp of terror and sprang off the sofa.
The pincushion sprang after him. Chase the dog!
Get the dog!

"Help!" cried Woffles. He tore into the hall.
The pincushion tore after him. Chase the dog! Get the dog!

Bang! went Woffles' head against the leg of the hall table.

Thud! went Woffles' heart against his ribcage, as he raced into the kitchen.

Woffles squeezed himself between the washing machine and the fridge. But even there he wasn't safe.

The pincushion leapt on to the washing machine and began slashing at him from above.

Woffles howled and tore off again. Up the hall, into the sitting room. Around the sofa, around the chairs. Chased by a spitting bundle of fur ...

And Stretch just very slightly opened an eye, closed it again, and went on snoozing.

But it was hard to sleep with such a noise going on. Thud, thump! Bang, bump!

Stretch twitched his whiskers, crossly. This was impossible!

Suddenly, everything went quiet. Stretch opened an eye.

Muffy was sitting on the sofa. She was washing herself and looking very pleased.

Stretch stood up on top of the television set. He yawned and he stretched. He stretched and he yawned. Then he leapt to the floor and went strolling out. He was king of the house!

But where was Woffles?

Woffles was under the kitchen table. He was shaking all over, like a jelly.

"This is *not* good enough," said Stretch, "a cat can have no peace in this house!"

Woffles hung his head.

"It's not your fault," said Stretch. "You're only a dog, after all. It takes a cat to deal with a cat. Leave it to me! I'll put a stop to this nonsense once and for all."

"But how?" whimpered Woffles.

"You'll see," said Stretch. He waved a paw. "Come with me."

Chapter 4

Woffles crawled out from under the kitchen table.
He was still frightened.

"Follow me," said Stretch.

Stretch led the way back up the hall.
Woffles crept behind.

Muffy was still sitting on the sofa, washing herself.

"I suppose you think you're really big and fierce?"
said Stretch.

Muffy smirked and went on washing.

"Well, let me tell you," said Stretch, "I know where
there's a MONSTER, just waiting to get you."

A Monster? Woffles began to shake all over again.

"Come upstairs," said Stretch, "I'll show you."

Up the stairs they went; Stretch, followed by Muffy, followed by Woffles.

"In there," said Stretch.

But that was the People's bedroom!

"We're n-not allowed to g-go in there," stammered Woffles.

"No," said Stretch, "and do you know why?"

Woffles shook his head.

"It's because there's a big, fierce MONSTER living in there," said Stretch.

"Ho," said Muffy, "I'm not scared of any monster!"

"Is that so?" said Stretch and he stre-e-e-e-tched up and opened the door. "Then I dare you to go in!"

Muffy hesitated.

"Scared?" asked Stretch.

"Not me!" said Muffy. And she went swaggering through the door ...

Woffles held his breath.

Suddenly there was a loud YOWL and Muffy came tearing out. She raced past Woffles and hurtled down the stairs. What could she have seen?

"Come," said Stretch to Woffles. "Come and look!"

Woffles didn't want to. He was frightened!

"Hold on to my tail," said Stretch. "We'll go in together."

So into the People's bedroom went Woffles and Stretch.

"Look!" said Stretch.

Woffles took a deep breath. He opened his eyes. There in front of him …

… stood a BIG WOOLLY DOG!

Chapter 5

When the People came home they found Woffles curled up on the sofa. He was fast asleep.

Stretch was stretched out on top of the television. He was fast asleep, too.

It had been a busy day!

"Where's Muffy?" asked the People. "Muffy! Muffy! Where are you, Muffy?"

They found her in the kitchen. She was crammed against the wall, between the washing machine and the fridge.

"Oh, poor Muffy!" cried the People. "What's frightened you?"

Muffy couldn't tell them it was the monster that lived in their bedroom. A hideous horrible thing like a big furry football with pins sticking out of it.

The People picked her up and carried her into the sitting room.

"There!" they said. "Go and cuddle Woffles. He'll look after you!"

So Muffy crept up to Woffles and burrowed into his fur. She made a little nest, where she could feel safe.

And Woffles let her! He could have growled and said, "Go away." But he didn't, because he wasn't that sort of dog.

Woffles wasn't frightened of Muffy any more. He'd seen the big woolly dog in the People's bedroom. No wonder Muffy had run away! Any cat would run from a big fierce dog like that!

Now Muffy always cuddles up with Woffles on the sofa. Muffy and Woffles do everything together. They even woffle around the garden together.

As for Stretch ... well! He just sleeps and eats and grooms and stretches. He never lifts a paw – why should he? He's king of the house!

Muffy meets a monster

Ideas for guided reading

Learning objectives: infer characters' feelings in fiction and consequences in logical explanations; write non-narrative texts, spell unfamiliar words; follow up others' points and show whether they agree or disagree; use the language of possibility to investigate and reflect on feelings behaviour and relationships; use some drama strategies to explore stories or issues; prepare stories for performance, identifying appropriate expression

Curriculum links: Citizenship: Children's rights - human rights

Interest words: creature, mite, pincushion, sweetie, bopped, snooze, mutt, torment, ribcage, terror, nonsense, hideous, crammed, grooms

Resources: writing materials, ICT

Getting started

This book can be read over two or more guided reading sessions.

- Ask children to look at the front cover and discuss what kind of story they think this is and why.

- Ask one of the children to read the blurb aloud. Explain to the children that they are going to read a story written from the animals' viewpoint.

- Discuss children's own experience of pets in the home. *Have they ever wondered how the world appears to their pets? Do their pets ever do funny things around the home?*

Reading and responding

- Ask children to read independently up to Chapter 3, suggesting that they make a note of tricky words to discuss later. Ask children why they think each of the animals behaves the way it does.

- Ask children to read quietly until the end of the book.